it's ok to cry

Story ©2020 Kimm Reid
Illustrations © 2020 Ahelia Publishing

Illustrations by Taralee Tilma

All rights reserved. No part of this work covered by the copyrights hereon may be reproduced or used in any form, or by any means—graphic, electronic, or mechanical—without the prior written permission of the publisher, including both the story and the illustrations.

ISBN #978-1-988001-49-4

Published in the United States of America

Printed in the United States of America

aheliapublishing@outlook.com

it's ok to cry

by Kimm Reid

(with the great help of sweet Annabelle)

illustrated by Taralee Tilma

Ahelia Publishing, LLC
Helena, Montana
USA

i am SAD

I was so sad, I started to cry.

My brother laughed at me, but I didn't care.

My heart was sad, and it made tears sneak out of my eyes.

I was playing with my favorite doll, Annabelle, but my sister pulled her from my hands and ran out of the house. I chased her down the stairs, but I couldn't catch up. She was bigger than me and could run faster. She took my sweet Annabelle and threw her into a tree so high that I couldn't reach to get her down.

My sister just laughed at me.

It made my heart hurt, and I cried for a long time. I thought I might never stop crying. I was so sad.

When my dad got home, he climbed up the tree and rescued Annabelle. I think she was sad too, but when I hugged her, she whispered to me.

"It's okay to be sad, I'm sad too. If something happens that hurts your heart, you must let it be sad for a little while, but don't give sadness any power. It can feel like your heart might break into a hundred pieces, and it's okay to let it hurt. It's okay to cry—but don't cry forever.

Don't let sadness be stronger than your heart.

Sadness can visit, but do not let it move in.

You own your SAD—your SAD does not own you."

i guess i'm the boss of my feelings ...

... my feelings aren't the boss of me.

So, like Annabelle said, I let my heart feel sad for a little while because, after all, my sweet dolly was all messed up from being in the tree. I straightened her dress and combed her hair, but she still had some smudges on her face … and a rip in her bow.

I felt sad for a few more minutes but then told the sadness it had to go. It couldn't have more power than me. I sniffled. I wiped my nose and dried my eyes. I started singing the happiest song I knew, and danced around with Annabelle.

If she could be happy, then I could be happy too.

I chose to be happy.

I chose to forgive my sister for being mean.

I chose to forgive my brother for laughing at me.

I said, "SAD, you cannot stay. You visited my heart,

but now it's time to go."

GOODBYE, SAD.

i am MAD

I was so mad, my head almost exploded.

My friend Violet said she would meet me at the park.

My mom said I could go, so Annabelle and I pulled on our sneakers

and ran to the park. We were so excited—

Violet was one of our favorite friends!

Well, not anymore.

When Annabelle and I were running to the park, we saw Violet and

Genevieve riding bikes. I waved, but Violet didn't stop.

She didn't wave. She didn't even go to the park.

I guess she was having more fun with her new friend.

I guess Violet lied.

I stomped all the way home and threw Annabelle on my bed.

I am so mad. I threw her too hard and she fell to the floor.

I ran to pick her up, but I was still so mad.

"I'm sorry, Annabelle," I said.

Now I felt mad at Violet for making me hurt Annabelle.

But Annabelle whispered to me.

"Violet didn't make you throw me. You chose to do that because you were mad with her. Sometimes it's hard to make good decisions when you're mad. Sometimes it's hard to remember we are mad at one person, and we become mean to another person.

It's okay to be mad. I'm mad too. Violet told you a lie. She didn't want to play with you today. She should have told you the truth. Maybe she already planned to ride bikes with Genevieve—you don't know. Maybe she didn't know how to do both things. Anyway, it's okay to be mad when someone tells you a lie. You can be mad and feel like being mean back. But don't. Don't let the mad stay. Don't give mad your power. Mad can visit, but do not let it move in.

You own your *mad*—your *mad* does not own you."

i guess i'm the boss of my feelings …

… my feelings aren't the boss of me.

I was mad for the whole day. Annabelle reminded me that mad had to go. It couldn't be stronger than me. So, I thought about it.

I wanted mad to stay.

It made me feel good to be mad.

Violet hurt my feelings, and I liked being mad at her.

But Annabelle was right.

Maybe Violet forgot she was going to meet me.

Maybe she didn't know what time it was.

Maybe Violet was with Genevieve because she was new to town and didn't have many friends.

Maybe she didn't see me.

I knew mad was only hurting me and Annabelle. After all, I threw her on the bed, and she fell to the floor.

I gave mad too much power and ended up hurting Annabelle.

So I straightened her dress and smoothed her hair,

but sweet Annabelle still looked a mess.

Maybe that's what mad looks like—a mess.

I felt mad for a few more minutes but then told the mad it couldn't stay—

it couldn't have any more power. I blinked my eyes hard until they stung.

Mad was stubborn; it didn't want to go. I sighed, then started singing the

happiest song I knew and danced around with Annabelle.

If she could be happy, then I could be happy too.

I chose to be happy.

I chose to forgive Violet for not keeping her promise.

I chose to forgive Genevieve for taking my friend's time.

I told Annabelle I was sorry for throwing her on the bed.

I said, "*mad*, you cannot stay. You visited my mind, but now you must go."

GOODBYE, MAD.

i am AFRAID

I was so afraid that I could hardly move.

My tongue felt weird. My mom and dad said goodnight hours ago

and I was supposed to be sleeping. But it was dark,

and I was scared of the dark.

I didn't know what was hiding in the dark.

When it was dark, everything was loud.

Noises I didn't hear in the light seemed loud in the dark.

I didn't know what was in the closet. I didn't know what was under the

bed. I got a little sweaty and I was afraid to close my eyes. I couldn't go

to sleep when I was so afraid. I kept trying hard to keep my eyes open,

even though I couldn't see. Even when they

started burning, I made them stay open.

It made my skin hurt and I could barely breathe.

I hugged Annabelle so close, I could hear her whisper.

"It's okay to be afraid. I'm afraid too.

It's very dark when the lights are off.

It's scary when the walls make funny sounds.

But there is nothing under the bed in the dark that's not there in the light.

There's nothing in the closet in the dark that's not there in the light.

Anyway, it's okay to be afraid when the lights are off. You can be afraid, and sometimes your skin hurts. Sometimes your tummy feels sick and your eyes burn. It's okay to feel afraid, but don't let it have any power.

Don't let fear stay. Have courage. You are stronger than fear.

Fear can visit, but do not let it move in.

You own your **FEAR**—your **FEAR** does not own you."

i guess i'm the boss of my feelings ...

... my feelings aren't the boss of me.

I felt afraid for a few more minutes because the dark was still there, but I told fear it couldn't stay.

I told fear it couldn't be stronger than me.

I pulled the blankets over my head and held Annabelle closer. I took a deep breath and let it out real slow and pretended I was pushing the fear out with the breaths. I imagined fear like a feather going over a waterfall. Compared to the waterfall, the feather had no power.

Compared to the truth, fear had no power either.

It took a lot of breaths, but Annabelle fell asleep.

If she could fall asleep, so could I.

If she could be courageous, then I could be too.

Very quietly, I sang the happiest song I knew and took my power back.

Fear couldn't have it.

I chose to have courage.

I chose to rest and believe the truth.

I chose to believe that nothing was in my closet in the dark

that wasn't there in the light.

I said, "FEAR, you cannot stay. You visited my soul, but now it's time to go."

GOODBYE, FEAR.

i am JEALOUS

I was so jealous! My cousin got a puppy.

I wanted a puppy. I told her a million trillion bazillion times I wanted a puppy, and I was going to name her Sophie the Marvelous. I begged my dad for a puppy,

but he said I wasn't old enough to take care of one.

My cousin is younger than me, but her dad let her get a puppy.

And guess what she named it?

My cousin named her puppy Sophie the Marvelous.

I didn't want to play with my cousin anymore because we'd have to play with Sophie the Marvelous and I wanted Sophie the Marvelous to belong to me.

She had a puppy and I didn't. When I got home, Sophie the Marvelous wouldn't come with me, because she wasn't mine.

My cousin got what I wanted, and I was jealous.

I didn't want to be her friend anymore. My insides were all twisted up like a knot because I was so jealous.

Maybe that was what jealousy looked like—a twisted up messy knot.

Annabelle held my hand and whispered to me.

"It's okay to feel jealous—for a minute. Someone got what you wanted. That's hard.

You can play with Sophie the Marvelous and love her and cuddle her.

Maybe your cousin thought if you weren't allowed to have Sophie the Marvelous, she would get her so you could still love her.

You don't really know why, so don't try to guess.

Think the best things, not the worst.

Thinking the worst things gives jealousy power.

Don't let jealous be more powerful than you.

Be happy that you can see Sophie the Marvelous sometimes. Sometimes is better than not at all.

Think of all the fun you and your cousin will have with Sophie the Marvelous.

Being jealous will steal your friendship.

Being jealous will hurt you and your cousin and Sophie the Marvelous.

It's not worth it. Jealousy can't have power.

Jealousy is a thief. It just steals everything and tells lies.

Jealousy can visit but do not let it move in.

You own your **JEALOUS**—your **JEALOUS** does not own you."

i guess i'm the boss of my feelings ...

... my feelings aren't the boss of me.

Annabelle was right.

It was better to love Sophie the Marvelous some of the time than not at all. I didn't know why my cousin got a puppy.

I didn't know why she named the puppy Sophie the Marvelous.

I guess I didn't need to know everything.

It wouldn't make a difference, since jealousy couldn't stay.

It couldn't have power.

I swung Annabelle around and started singing the happiest song I knew.

I forgave my cousin for having what I wanted.

I forgave her for naming the puppy Sophie the Marvelous.

I closed my eyes and dreamed of one day having a puppy of my own, but for now, I would play with her puppy.

I chose to be okay with that.

I decided to let that be enough.

I chose to be happy for her, and happy for me.

I chased jealousy away because it was not good for me to keep it.

It couldn't be stronger than me.

"JEALOUS, you cannot stay. You visited my heart, but now it's time to go."

GOODBYE, JEALOUS.

i am LONELY

Oh, I was so lonely.

It made my heart hurt quite a lot.

My cousin had Sophie the Marvelous to play with.

My friend Violet was busy with Genevieve.

My dad was working in the shop.

Annabelle was getting her bow fixed, and mom said she had to go in the wash.

I had nobody to play with, and I felt lonely.

It felt a little like sadness, and a little like madness, but different.

Like a piece of me was missing, or lost, or sleeping.

Like I was all alone in the great big world.

It whispered lies, like "You're not important."

There were lots of things I could do.

I liked to draw, or I could play with my other toys.

I didn't like playing alone though. Instead, I was thinking about how lonely I was.

The more I thought about it, the lonelier I felt.

I wished I had Annabelle to tell me what to do.

But I supposed if I had Annabelle, I wouldn't be lonely.

I sat down on my bed to think about how lonely I was.

Instead, I started to wonder about Annabelle and what she might say. She was very wise, Annabelle was. She knew things I didn't know about feelings and power and what was true and what wasn't.

She taught me how to tell my feelings to leave me alone.

I wished everyone could have an Annabelle.

Oh, how I missed her. Oh, how lonely I felt without her.

Annabelle would probably say:

"It's okay to be lonely, I'm lonely too.

When you're all alone and it hurts your heart, you must let it feel hurt

for a little while, but don't let it have any power.

It can feel like you'll be alone forever, but you won't.

It feels like you're not important, but you are.

It feels like you don't matter, but you do.

It can feel like you're a little lost, but you're not.

It's okay to feel lonely—but not forever.

Don't let lonely be more powerful than you.

Loneliness can visit, but do not let it move in.

You own your Lonely—your Lonely does not own you."

i guess i'm the boss of my feelings ...

... my feelings aren't the boss of me.

I let myself feel lonely for a few more minutes, but then I chased it away.

The longer I let it stay, the harder it was to make it go.

The longer it whispered to me, the more power it had.

Instead, I thought about all the people who loved me. Just because they were away now, didn't mean they didn't love me. They were just busy today.

That was okay.

I decided to play make-believe with other toys. I played with Annabelle so much, I wondered if maybe some of the other toys felt lonely too.

We played tea party and hide and seek.

We told secrets and giggled.

I noticed the lonely was gone. It couldn't stay. It had no power.

"Lonely, you cannot stay. You visited my heart, but now it's time to go."

Goodbye, Lonely.

i am HAPPY

I felt so happy, I could sing and dance all day.

Maybe I would.

Not everything was perfect.

Annabelle lost a shoe and her hair was all tangled,

but she was still beautiful.

Violet moved away, so I didn't get to see her anymore,

but I'd make new friends. Genevieve was nice.

I still didn't have a puppy named Sophie the Marvelous.

I checked my closet and under my bed before I went to

sleep now, because I knew there was nothing there in the

dark that wasn't there in the light.

I still get so SAD that I cry and cry, but that's okay.

It is okay to cry.

I sometimes get so MAD that it feels like my head might explode.

Once in a while, I get very JEALOUS, but not enough to give it power.

Last week, I felt LONELY when Annabelle had to go in the wash,

but I played with other things.

I am not happy because everything is perfect.

I am happy because Annabelle taught me how to be happy.

She taught me how to have power over my feelings and choose

which ones get to stay, and which ones have to go.

I still feel my feelings when they come, because they are important.

But I don't give them power, and they cannot stay.

I am happy because I choose to be happy.

I wish everyone could have an Annabelle. She is very wise.

So, I choose to be HAPPY.

I choose to be kind because being kind is important.

I choose to sing the happiest song I know, no matter what my heart feels like, and I choose to dance all over the room with sweet Annabelle.

I am proud that I learned to not give away my power.

I am glad I learned I was in charge of my feelings.

I am excited I learned it is good to feel our feelings and to think about our feelings and to understand our feelings.

Sometimes, our thoughts tell us lies and try convince us to let bad feelings stay. Sometimes the feelings don't want to go. But we must chase them away so the good feelings can come in their place.

Happy feelings and sad feelings can't stay at the same time for long.

We must choose one or the other.

It's our choice.

We must think about our feelings

but not let our feelings

tell us how to think.

We are courageous when we chase bad feelings away.

We are wise when we choose good feelings even though

the bad ones want to stay.

We are brave when we apologize. We are braver when

we forgive. We are the most brave when we forgive

people who aren't even sorry!

Be courageous.

Be wise.

Be brave.

Cry if you must, but don't cry forever.

remember,

you are the boss of your feelings ...

... your feelings are not the boss of you.

Printed in the USA
CPSIA information can be obtained
at www.ICGtesting.com
LVHW071242171023
761168LV00035B/617